This book belongs to:

....

For Seb, Pippa and Harry

OXFORD
UNIVERSITY PRESS

Great Clarendon Street, Oxford OX2 6DP

Oxford University Press is a department of the University of Oxford. It furthers the University's objective of excellence in research, scholarship, and education by publishing worldwide. Oxford is a registered trade mark of Oxford University Press in the UK and in certain other countries

First published 2019

British Library Cataloguing in Publication Data
Data available

ISBN: 978-0-19-276758-5

10 9 8 7 6 5 4 3 2 1

Printed in China

Paper used in the production of this book is a natural, recyclable product made from wood grown in sustainable forests. The manufacturing process conforms to the environmental regulations of the country of origin.

CYRiL

THE LONELY CLOUD

tim hopgood

OXFORD
UNIVERSITY PRESS

'Let's have a picnic!'

Everyone agreed it was a
perfect day for a picnic.

At least it was until Cyril turned up.

It was sad but
true, no one was
ever pleased
to see Cyril.

He was always
being blamed
for ruining
everyone's fun.

All Cyril wanted was to look down on the world and see a **happy** smile.

The trouble was, he knew what
everyone was thinking . . .

*I wish that cloud
would go away!*

So that's exactly
what he did.

Cyril drifted far, far away in
search of a friendly face.

He floated over farmland,
rivers and bridges . . .

above towns

and famous cities . . .

and over the **ocean** too!

As Cyril drifted across
the water he gradually
became **bigger** . . .

and
bigger!

Eventually Cyril came to a new land.

The ground was **baking** hot.

But as
Cyril drifted
slowly across
the sky . . .

his **huge**
shadow cooled
the earth.

Everyone seemed to welcome
the **shade** that Cyril gave.

This made
Cyril feel
so happy
that he cried.

Not tears of
sadness . . .

but big,
big tears of
glorious joy!

As Cyril's tears soaked the land,

everything seemed to smile!

And that
was all
Cyril
had ever
wanted . . .

to look
down
on the
world
and
see a
happy
smile.